Please return/renew this item by the last date
shown. Books may be renewed by
telephoning, writing to or calling in at any
library or on the Internet.

Northamptonshire Libraries and Information Service

Northamptonshire
County Council

www.northamptonshire.gov.uk/leisure/libraries/

For Willoughby Cooke,
who listened to me telling stories
on October 13, 2008
S.G.

For Oscar
J.B.

ORCHARD BOOKS
338 Euston Road, London NW1 3BH

Orchard Books Australia

Hachette Children's Books
Level 17/207 Kent Street, Sydney NSW 2000

First published by Orchard Books in 2009
First paperback publication in 2010

A CIP catalogue record for this book is available from the British Library.
All rights reserved.

ISBN 978 1 84616 109 4 (hardback)
ISBN 978 1 84616 159 9 (paperback)

1 3 5 7 9 10 8 6 4 2 (hardback)
1 3 5 7 9 10 8 6 4 2 (paperback)

Printed in China

Orchard Books is a division of Hachette Children's Books,
an Hachette UK company.

www.hachette.co.uk

THE BEAR DETECTIVES

Who Shouted Boo?

Written by **SALLY GRINDLEY**
Illustrated by **JO BROWN**

ORCHARD BOOKS

Constable Tiggs

Sergeant Bumble

Mother Gabble

Mr Pink

Mrs Nibble

Sergeant Bumble and Constable
Tiggs were driving round the
village, when they saw a rabbit
with her fur standing up on end.

They stopped the car and went over to her. She was shaking like a jelly.

"Are you all right,
Mrs Nibble?" asked Bumble.

"You look as if
you've seen a
ghost," said Tiggs.

"I was walking along, thinking about my supper, when someone shouted, 'BOO!' It frightened the life out of me," said Mrs Nibble.

"Wow!" said Tiggs. "That's serious!"
"Very serious," said Bumble, "but
nothing we can't handle.
Take your notepad and pencil,
Constable Tiggs, and we
will investigate."

They
walked slowly
up and down the path.

"Let's see if anyone is hiding behind
the bushes," whispered Tiggs.
They crept behind the bushes,
but there was nobody there.

They were about to
examine the grass for clues,
when they heard a loud

"*OINK!*"

They ran out from behind the
bushes. There was a pig with his
tail sticking straight up on end
instead of being curly.

He was shaking like a jelly.

"Are you
all right,
Mr Pink?"
asked Bumble.

"Was it a BOO?" asked Tiggs.
"Right in the middle of my song,"
said Mr Pink. "Oink, oink, oinkety,
snort, snort, then BOO!"

"Wow! That's serious!" said Tiggs.
"Very serious," said Bumble. "Don't
worry, Mr Pink, we will catch the
culprit who spoilt your song."

"Let's look behind that fence," said
Tiggs. They crept behind the fence,
but there was nobody there.

"A clue!" cried Tiggs. "Somebody has left a sweet wrapper on the ground." "That somebody must like sweets, then," Bumble declared importantly.

Just then a loud HONK HONK
HONK! made Bumble jump up in
the air. He landed on Tiggs's toes.
"YOW!" yelled Tiggs, hopping
up and down.
"Terribly sorry, Constable Tiggs,"
said Bumble.

They ran out from behind the fence and saw a goose with her feathers sticking up on end. She was shaking like a jelly.

"What happened, Mother Gabble?" asked Bumble. "I was waddling along, wondering where to lay my next egg, when someone shouted,

'BOO!'

It frightened the life out of me."

Bumble and Tiggs looked at each
other in astonishment.
"But who would dare to shout
'BOO!' to a goose?" they said.

They looked all around but there
was nobody to be seen. Then they
heard a giggle. It was coming from
behind a line of washing.

24

"There are legs sticking out from
under those sheets," whispered Tiggs.
"So there are," whispered Bumble.
They crept over to the washing line.

With one quick movement they
lifted up the sheets. Behind them
stood five small bears.
"Would you like a sweet?"
one of them asked shyly.
"Who shouted BOO?" asked
Bumble sternly.

"I did," giggled the smallest bear.
"They said I wouldn't say BOO
to a goose, so I did."
"And to a rabbit and a pig
as well?" asked Tiggs.
The little bear nodded.

"Frightening people is a serious
matter," said Bumble.
"Very serious," said Tiggs.

"I think you need to go and say
sorry," said Bumble.
"Yes, Sir, Sergeant Bumble, Sir,"
said the bears, and off they ran.

"That's another mystery solved,
then," said Tiggs.
"Indeed," said Bumble. "And now
it's time for a nice cup of tea."

THE BEAR DETECTIVES

SALLY GRINDLEY & JO BROWN

Bucket Rescue	978 1 84616 152 0
Who Shouted Boo?	978 1 84616 109 4
The Ghost Train	978 1 84616 153 7
Treasure Hunt	978 1 84616 108 7
The Mysterious Earth	978 1 84616 155 1
The Strange Pawprint	978 1 84616 156 8
The Missing Spaghetti	978 1 84616 157 5
A Very Important Day	978 1 84616 154 4

All priced at £8.99

Orchard Colour Crunchies are available from all good bookshops,
or can be ordered direct from the publisher:
Orchard Books, PO BOX 29, Douglas IM99 1BQ
Credit card orders please telephone 01624 836000
or fax 01624 837033 or visit our website: www.orchardbooks.co.uk
or e-mail: bookshop@enterprise.net for details.

To order please quote title, author and ISBN
and your full name and address.
Cheques and postal orders should be made payable to 'Bookpost plc.'
Postage and packing is FREE within the UK
(overseas customers should add £2.00 per book).

Prices and availability are subject to change.